But Not Gino

By Shari Lyon
Art by Lee Kohse

Blue Sneaker
Press

Blue Sneaker
Press

But Not Gino was published by Blue Sneaker Press. Blue Sneaker works with authors, illustrators, nonprofit organizations, and corporations to publish children's books that engage, entertain, and educate kids on subjects that affect our world. Blue Sneaker Press is an imprint of Southwestern Publishing Group, Inc., 2451 Atrium Way, Nashville, Tennessee, 37214. Southwestern Publishing Group is a wholly owned subsidary of Southwestern/Great American, Inc., Nashville, Tennessee.

Christopher G. Capen, president, Southwestern Publishing Group
www.swpublishinggroup.com • 800-358-0560 • ccapen@swpublishinggroup.com

ISBN: 978-1-943198-00-9
Library of Congress Control Number: 2015941141

Printed in China
10 9 8 7 6 5 4 3 2 1

First published in 2013 by Cozy Lyon Press.

To my Grandies,
who always make me feel tall
and put a song in my heart.

—Shari

For my little boy, Juan.
Keep drawing. Keep dreaming.

—Lee

All giraffes are tall. Everyone knows that. Well, most giraffes are tall.

But not Gino.

Gino was a short giraffe.

The tall giraffes could stretch their necks to get the tender new leaves that grew high up on the trees.

But not Gino.

He had to settle for the tough leaves close to the middle of the trees and the leftovers that fell to the ground.

The tall giraffes could see danger coming from far away because they could see above the heads of the other animals on the savanna.

But not Gino.

He had to wait with the other herd animals for the tall giraffes to warn them that danger was coming.

The tall giraffes could hang out together face-to-face while they stood in the shade of the tall trees.

But not Gino.

He didn't like to hang out much.
Gino liked to sing.

One afternoon after the herds had all visited
the water hole, Gino went off by himself to
stand beside a tall termite mound that was
near a big boulder so he could sing to himself.

"I know I'm small
But maybe tall enough.
Tall enough to share a smile.
Tall enough to play a game.
Tall enough to be a friend to you—
To stand beside you in the rain."

"I know I'm small
But maybe tall enough.
Tall enough to share a story.
Tall enough to wish you well.
Tall enough to hum a tune to you
On this lovely sunshine day."

When Gino finished singing his song, he smiled and leaned his head on the big, warm boulder beside him. Gino closed his eyes. Before long, Gino heard voices. Was he dreaming? Gino opened his eyes.

Peeking around the rock were the faces of some of the young animals—a wildebeest, impala, zebra, and even a springbok.

"Why did you stop singing, Gino?" asked the young wildebeest. "We were almost asleep when you stopped."

"Yes," added the impala, "please sing your song again."

Gino blinked his eyes a few times to make sure he was really awake.

"Really?" Gino asked. "Do you like my song?"

"Yes!" the young animals all said at once.

"Hmmm," said Gino. He had never thought of anyone else liking his singing. So Gino sang his song again.

"I know I'm small
But maybe tall enough.
Tall enough to share a smile.
Tall enough to play a game.
Tall enough to be a friend to you—
To stand beside you in the rain."

"I know I'm small
But maybe tall enough.
Tall enough to share a story.
Tall enough to wish you well.
Tall enough to hum a tune to you
On this lovely sunshine day."

When his song was over, Gino looked behind
the big boulder. Sure enough, the young animals were all there . . . sound asleep.

Gino started to walk around
the boulder to sit beside his friends,
but he was stopped in his tracks by the
scratchy voice of a father wildebeest.

"How did you do that, Gino?" he asked.

"I just sang to them," Gino said.

"I am so glad. We have a long walk ahead of us tomorrow to find a new water hole. It's good that the young ones are getting a nice rest today, but I didn't know giraffes could make sounds, let alone sing!" said the father wildebeest.

"Of course giraffes
can make sounds," Gino said.
"The tall giraffes have long
necks, so their voices sound too low
for most other animals to hear.
You are right about the singing, though.
I don't think I have ever heard the tall giraffes sing."

"Well, how about that!" the father wildebeest said. "You learn something new every day." And with a quick smile, a flick of his tail, and a toss of his great head, the wildebeest walked back to join the rest of the herd animals.

Gino stood up and realized that he felt a little bit taller. He walked between the big boulder and the tall termite mound. "Hmmm," said Gino. "I may be a small giraffe, but I think I am tall enough for the important things."

And then, feeling quite content, Gino stretched up to his full height and walked back to join the tall giraffes. It was time to sing his song to them.

"I know I'm small
But maybe tall enough.
Tall enough to share a smile.
Tall enough to play a game.
Tall enough to be a friend to you—
To stand beside you in the rain."

"I know I'm small
But maybe tall enough.
Tall enough to share a story.
Tall enough to wish you well.
Tall enough to hum a tune to you
On this lovely sunshine day."

From that day on, Gino and the tall giraffes were friends, and they often joined him when he sang his song.

GINO'S SONG
Music and Lyrics by Shari Lyon
Copyright 2013 by Shari Lyon

"I know I'm small
But maybe tall enough.
Tall enough to share a smile.
Tall enough to play a game.
Tall enough to be a friend to you—
To stand beside you in the rain."

"I know I'm small
But maybe tall enough.
Tall enough to share a story.
Tall enough to wish you well.
Tall enough to hum a tune to you
On this lovely sunshine day."

Gino's Song

Words & Music by Shari Lyon

Fun Facts About Giraffes

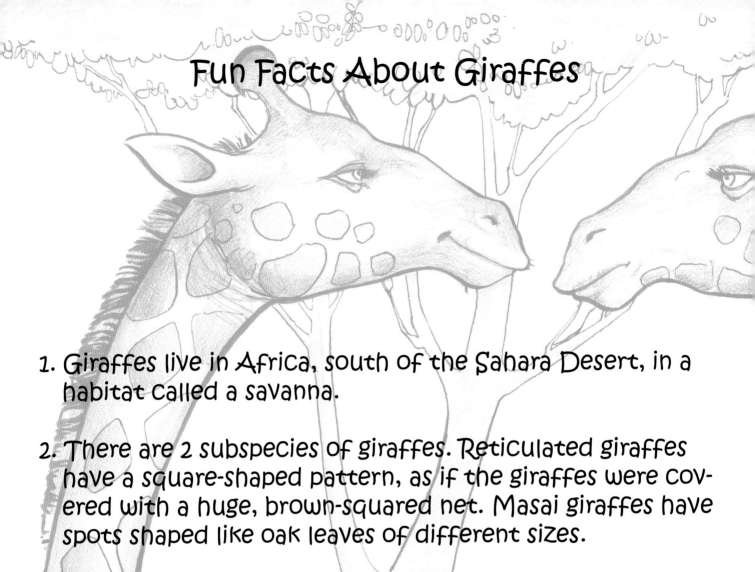

1. Giraffes live in Africa, south of the Sahara Desert, in a habitat called a savanna.

2. There are 2 subspecies of giraffes. Reticulated giraffes have a square-shaped pattern, as if the giraffes were covered with a huge, brown-squared net. Masai giraffes have spots shaped like oak leaves of different sizes.

3. Giraffes eat the leaves of the Acacia tree.

4. Giraffes have long, tough, bluish purple tongues covered with bristly hair to help them eat the thorny Acacia leaves.

5. Giraffes are the tallest land animals and can look right into a 2-story building without even stretching their necks!

6. Male giraffes can be about 18 feet tall. Females stand about 14 feet tall. Baby giraffes are about 6 feet tall when they are born!

7. Both male and female giraffes have 2 small hair-covered horns called ossicones. They use them to playfully fight with one another.

8. A giraffe's feet are about the same size as a dinner plate.

9. Although a giraffe's neck is about 6 feet (1.8 meters) long, it has the same number of vertebrae as a human's neck.

10. Female giraffes give birth standing up, so their babies fall 6 feet to the ground before they take their first breath!

About the Creators

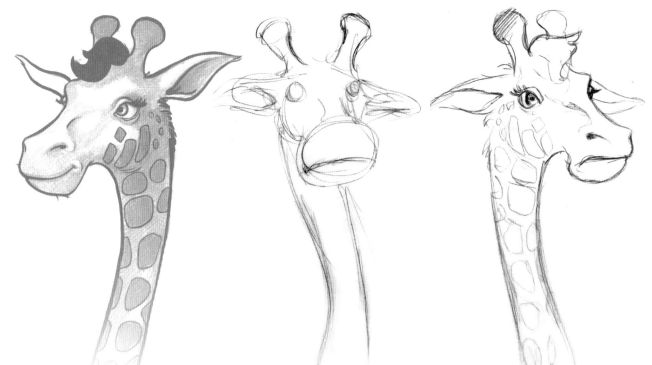

SHARI LYON: Author, actress, playwright, teacher, and musician, she lives in Escondido, California—just a few miles from the San Diego Zoo's Safari Park—with her husband, Neil. Shari loves children and animals.

LEE KOHSE: Artist and illustrator, he lives in San Diego, California—not too far from the world famous San Diego Zoo—with his wife, Maria, and his son, Juan. Lee has created art for *Speed Racer*, *Star Wars*, and *The Lord of the Rings*. See more of his art at www.kohse.com.